7

The
Lightning
Bugs

OTHER IKE AND MEM STORIES

The Bird Shadow

The Tornado Watches

The Weeping Willow

THE LIGHTNING BUGS

An Ike and Mem Story

BY Patrick Jennings

ILLUSTRATED BY
Anna Alter

HOLIDAY HOUSE / NEW YORK

Text copyright © 2003 by Patrick Jennings
Illustrations copyright © 2003 by Anna Alter
All Rights Reserved
Printed in the United States of America
The text typeface is Hightower.
The jacket art is watercolor and colored pencil.
The black-and-white interior illustrations
are pen and ink using Pigma Micron drawing pens.
www.holidayhouse.com
First Edition

Library of Congress Cataloging-in-Publication Data
Jennings, Patrick.
The lightning bugs / by Patrick Jennings ; illustrated by Anna Alter.—1st ed.
p. cm.
"An Ike and Mem story."
Summary: Ike feels bad about not saying anything
to neighborhood bully Dave when Dave insists
on killing lightning bugs to separate
their glowing parts from their bodies
to make "lightning rings"
for the other children's fingers.
ISBN 0-8234-1673-9 (hardcover)
[1. Fireflies—Fiction. 2. Bullies—Fiction.]
I. Alter, Anna, ill. II. Title.
PZ7.J4298715 Li 2003
[Fic]—dc21   2002032729

For Aunt Ruth,
salt of the earth
—P. J.

It was the middle of summer, and Ike and his little sister, Mem, were playing in the backyard with some friends. Ike's best friend and next-door neighbor, Buzzy, was there and so was Dave Hove and his little brother, Hugo. The sun had just gone down, and lightning bugs were floating in the air like sparks.

Mem caught one in her cupped palms and put it into an empty mayonnaise jar. The jar's lid had small holes in it that Ike had punched with a nail.

Ike and Buzzy and Hugo caught lightning

bugs too. They put them into the jar with Mem's. The jar glowed like a lantern.

Dave also caught a lightning bug, but he didn't put it into the jar. He ripped it in half. Then he pressed the lightning part of the bug onto the back of his finger. It still glowed.

"Look!" he said to Ike and Buzzy. "A lightning ring!" He waved his hand at them.

"Ew," Hugo said, sticking out his tongue.

Mem walked up to Dave and said, "Don't kill the lightning bugs, Dave!"

Dave just snatched another one from the air and tore off its lightning part.

"Stop!" Mem yelled.

"Here, Buzzy," Dave said, smiling. "Have a lightning ring."

Buzzy didn't look like he wanted a light-

ning ring. But he took it. He pressed it onto the back of his finger.

"Buzzy!" Mem yelled. "That's disgusting. Take it off!"

Buzzy didn't say anything. He turned his hand over so he couldn't see the lightning ring.

Dave caught another bug and tore off its lightning part.

"Stop it! Stop it!" Mem yelled, stamping her feet.

"Here, Ike," Dave said. "One for you too."

Ike didn't want it. But he took it. He pressed it onto the back of his finger.

"IKE!" Mem yelled. "You big dummy!" She gave him a shove, then stomped away.

Ike didn't like her to call him that, or to shove him, especially in front of the guys. But most of all he didn't like the way he was feeling. He looked down at the lightning ring on his finger. He turned his hand over so he couldn't see it.

Dave caught another lightning bug and tore it apart.

"Here you go, Hugo," he said. "Have a lightning ring just like the big guys."

"Gross," Hugo said. He put his hands behind his back.

Then a voice called out, "Da-vid! Hu-go!" It was Mrs. Hove's voice.

"Coming, Mom!" Dave shouted.

He gave his hand a shake. His lightning ring flew off and landed in the grass.

"See you guys later," he said, then walked off toward home. Hugo followed behind.

Ike turned his hand over and looked at the lightning ring. It was still glowing.

Buzzy looked at his. It was glowing too. He shook it off, and it landed in the grass.

"I'm going home," he said. Then he ran next door.

Ike shook the lightning ring off his finger too. It landed in the grass near Buzzy's and Dave's. A yellow-green spot glowed on his finger. He licked his thumb and rubbed the spot. It didn't come off. He rubbed it on his shirt. The spot wouldn't come off.

Ike picked up the mayonnaise jar and unscrewed the lid. The lightning bugs' wings opened and, one by one, the bugs flew out. They flew around Ike in a circle. They made a lightning ring around him. He set down the jar and ran inside as fast as he could.

Ike climbed the stairs two at a time. He ran down the hall to the bathroom. He tried to wash off the yellow-green spot with soap. It wouldn't wash off. He tried to scrub it off with a washcloth. It wouldn't scrub off. He took out a box of plastic bandages from the medicine cabinet. He unwrapped a bandage and wrapped it around the spot.

"Don't kill the lightning bugs, Dave!" he heard Mem say in a high voice.

"I can kill as many as I want," she said in a low voice.

"Then I will call the police," she said in a high voice. "Hello, police? This is Mem. I want to report that Dave is killing lightning bugs."

"You squealer!" she said in a low voice.

Ike tiptoed down the hall to the playroom and peeked inside. Mem was sitting on the floor with some of her stuffed animals. Gina the bunny and Stinky the skunk were in her lap. Mem was holding her toy phone up to Gina's ear.

"The police are coming right over," she said in a high voice.

Gina is Mem, Ike thought.

Mem put down the phone. She picked up Stinky.

"They can't make me stop," she said in a low voice.

Stinky is Dave, Ike thought.

"You make him stop, Ike," she said in a high voice.

Ike jumped. He thought she was talking to him. But she was still just pretending. She put down the skunk and picked up Toady the toad.

"I don't want to," she said in a croaky voice.

Toady is me, Ike thought.

Ike tiptoed away to his room. He didn't turn on the light. He walked to the window. He saw the lightning rings glowing in the grass. He saw lightning bugs floating in the dark sky. He pulled the curtains closed.

The next morning Ike went into the bathroom. In the mirror he saw the bandage on his finger. He had forgotten all about it. He had forgotten all about the lightning rings.

He thought about peeling off the bandage to see if the yellow-green spot was still there. But he didn't peel it off. He didn't want to see the spot.

Mem was sitting at the kitchen table eating cereal when Ike went down for breakfast. He stuffed his left hand—the one with the bandage—into his pocket.

"Hi, Mem," he said.

Mem didn't look up from her bowl. She scooped a spoonful of cornflakes into her mouth and crunched it loudly.

Ike decided he didn't want breakfast. He had a knot in his stomach. He walked past Mem to the back door. He stepped out onto the porch and looked out at the grass. He couldn't see any lightning rings in it.

He went into the garage and wheeled out the lawn mower. He pulled the cord and the motor started. Then he mowed the backyard.

When he shut off the motor, a voice from behind him said, "Good morning, Ike." It was his mother's voice.

"Oh, hi, Mom," Ike said, stuffing his left hand into his pocket.

"Today is Thursday, you know," his mother said.

"I know," Ike said.

"Usually you mow on Saturday."

"I know. I just felt like mowing."

His mother smiled. "Okay," she said. "Thank you."

"You're welcome," Ike said. Then he pushed the lawn mower away with one hand. He kept the other one in his pocket.

"Is there something wrong with your hand?" his mother asked.

"No," Ike said. "I just feel like pushing with one hand."

"Okay," his mother said.

Ike went into the house for his mitt and his bat. He didn't see Mem anywhere. He was glad.

As he was passing through the kitchen on his way back outside, his mother stopped him.

"Will you pick up a few things for me on the way home?" she asked.

Ike set down his bat and stuffed his left hand into his pocket. "Sure," he said.

"We need a gallon of milk and a loaf of bread," she said, and held out a ten-dollar bill.

Ike set down his mitt, took the money,

stuffed it into his pocket, then picked up his mitt again.

"Are you sure there's nothing wrong with your hand?" his mother asked.

"I'm sure," Ike said.

When his mother left the room, Ike took his hand out of his pocket and picked up his bat. He went out to the garage, tied his gear into his bike basket, then wheeled his bike out onto the driveway. Mem was playing in the sandbox with her little people.

"This is what happens when you kill lightning bugs, Dave," she said. She pushed Ike's bulldozer through the sand and covered up one of the little people.

"No, Mem!" she said in a low voice. "I'll never do it again! I promise!"

She dug the little person out of the sand.

"Then you can drive the bulldozer," she said. She set the little person in the bulldozer seat.

Ike rolled his bike down the driveway and pedaled away.

Ike rode next door to Buzzy's house. He rang the doorbell, then stuffed his left hand into his pocket. Buzzy opened the door. His left hand was in his pocket too.

"You ready?" Ike asked.

"Yeah," Buzzy said. "Just let me get my gear."

Buzzy got his mitt and bat and tied them into his bike basket with one hand. Then he and Ike rode one-handed to the baseball field.

The Hoves' bikes were lying in the grass.

Dave was hitting pop flies to Hugo, but they kept falling on the grass around him.

Ike and Buzzy got off their bikes and set their kickstands. They both untied their gear one-handed. Then they both pulled their hands out of their pockets and quickly stuffed them into their mitts.

"Finally!" Dave called out. "Some *real* outfielders!"

Hugo sighed and sat down on the grass.

Dave hit flies to Ike and Buzzy. After a while he yelled, "I'm sick of batting! One of you guys come in and hit!"

Ike didn't want to hit. Batting required two hands.

"I just want to shag flies," he yelled to Dave.

"So do I!" yelled Buzzy.

"Then I'm leaving!" Dave yelled.

He picked up his gear and walked over to his bike. Hugo stood up and walked to his.

"See you guys tonight!" Dave yelled as he and Hugo rode away. "I'll make you more lightning rings!"

Ike and Buzzy sighed and sat down on the grass. A bug fluttered around them, then landed on Ike's mitt.

"It's a lightning bug," Ike said.

"But they don't come out during the day," Buzzy said.

"Yes, they do," Ike said.

"No, they don't," Buzzy said.

"Yes, they do," Ike said.

They both sat quietly for a minute. Then

Buzzy said, "I don't like Dave's dumb lightning rings."

"Me neither," Ike said.

The bug on his mitt opened its wings and flew away.

Buzzy rode with Ike to the supermarket. He sat with the bikes while Ike went in. Ike got a gallon of milk and a loaf of bread, then he got in the shortest checkout line. Debbie Antcliff's mother was in front of him. Debbie Antcliff was Mem's best friend at school.

"Hello, Ike," Mrs. Antcliff said. "Why, what's happened to your finger?"

Ike was holding the gallon of milk with his left hand.

"Nothing really," he said.

"I was just at your house, dropping off Debbie," Mrs. Antcliff said. "Your mother invited her for dinner and a sleepover."

Ike nodded. He'd forgotten about that.

Mrs. Antcliff paid for her groceries. "Good-bye, Ike," she said. "I hope your finger gets better soon."

"Thanks," Ike said.

He put the milk and bread on the moving belt. He paid the cashier with his mother's money and took his change. The bag girl put the groceries in a brown paper bag. Ike picked it up and walked toward the automatic doors.

Next to the doors were new red gum ball machines. On the front of one of them were pictures of bugs, snakes, toads, and spiders, and the words:

GLOW-IN-THE-DARK

CREEPY-CRAWLY RINGS!

10¢

Ike peered through the glass. He saw lots of colored gum balls. He also saw some clear plastic containers. In the containers were yellow-green rings with yellow-green creepy-crawlies attached.

Ike reached into his pocket. He felt the change from the milk and bread. It was his mother's change. He pulled out a dime and started to put it in the gum ball machine's slot. Then he stopped. It was his mother's dime. He put it back in his pocket and went out through the automatic doors.

Ike and Buzzy rode home one-handed. Mem
and Debbie Antcliff were playing in the backyard in the sprinkler.

"Hi, Mem! Hi, Debbie!" Ike called out as
he set his kickstand.

Mem and Debbie pretended not to hear him.

"Still sore at you, huh?" Buzzy said.

"I guess so," Ike said. "Look, I have to bring
in the groceries and give my mom her change.
And she has some chores for me to do."

"Okay," Buzzy said. "See you after supper."
And he pedaled away.

Ike put away the groceries and set his mother's change on the kitchen counter. He took a butter knife out of the silverware drawer, slipped it into his back pocket, and covered the handle with his T-shirt. Then he tiptoed up to his room, closed his door, and locked it.

He set his piggy bank on his bed, slid the butter knife blade into the bank's slot, then turned the bank upside down. A nickel and two pennies dropped out. He shook the bank again and more coins dropped out. He kept shaking it until there were twenty dimes on the bedspread. He stuffed them into his front pocket, slid the nickels and pennies back into the bank, and put the bank away. Then he unlocked his door and ran down the stairs two at a time. He ran through the house and out the back door.

Mem and Debbie were sitting at the picnic table, wrapped in big towels, playing Chutes and Ladders.

"Who's winning?" Ike asked.

"I am," Debbie said with a grin.

Mem gave Debbie a look. Debbie stopped grinning. Mem flicked the spinner with a hard snap.

Ike rode two-handed to the supermarket. He went straight to the creepy-crawly gum ball machine. He pulled a dime out of his pocket, slid it into the slot, and turned the handle. There was a *clink,* and he lifted the little silver door. A green gum ball tumbled into his hand. He stuffed it into his front pocket, put another dime in the slot, and turned the handle. There was another *clink.* He lifted the silver door, and an orange gum ball tumbled out. He stuffed it into his pocket with the green one.

Then he put another dime in the slot, turned the handle, and a blue gum ball tumbled out. He stuffed it into his pocket with the others, put another dime in the slot, and turned the handle. A clear plastic container tumbled out. Inside it was a yellow-green spider ring.

Ike set the container on top of the gum ball machine and put another dime in the slot. He turned the handle: orange gum ball. He stuffed it into his pocket. He put in another dime and turned the handle: plastic container. This one had a yellow-green beetle ring inside. He set it next to the spider ring, then dug out his dimes. He had fourteen left. It had taken him six dimes to get two rings. He needed four more rings. Would he have enough dimes? It was like a word problem in math. Ike hated word problems.

He put in eight more dimes and got five more gum balls and three more rings: a snake, a slug, and another beetle. He only needed one more. He put a dime in the slot and a yellow gum ball tumbled out. He put four more dimes in and got four more gum balls. He stuffed them into his back pockets. The front ones were full.

There were now five rings on top of the machine. He needed six. He closed his eyes, made a secret wish, then put his last dime in the slot.

It bounced out. There was a *bling*, as if it hit the floor, then it disappeared.

Ike dropped to his hands and knees and started hunting for it.

"Hey, kid," a voice above him said. "Lose something?"

Ike looked up. It was the bag girl.

"I dropped my last dime," Ike said.

"Oh yeah?" the bag girl said. "Here, I'll help you look."

They looked under the shopping carts and the floor waxers. They looked under the newspaper racks. The bag girl looked behind the checkout counters.

"I'm sorry, kid," she said. "I just don't see it any—" She pointed at Ike's foot. "Look!" she said.

Ike looked down at his foot. The dime was peeking out of his tennis shoe! He bent over and picked it out.

"Thanks," he said to the bag girl. He dug a handful of gum balls out of his back pocket. "Want one?"

"Okay," she said. She took a blue one and

popped it into her mouth. "Thanks."

"Sure," Ike said, stuffing the rest back into his pocket. "I have a lot."

"So?" the bag girl said. "What are you waiting for?" She gave Ike a nudge with her elbow.

He smiled and ran back to the gum ball machine. He carefully put the dime into the slot, then turned the handle. There was a *clink*. He lifted the silver door.

A green gum ball tumbled into his hand.

"It's not your lucky day," the bag girl said from behind him.

Ike didn't turn around. He just stared at the machine. His face felt hot.

"Here," the bag girl said. She reached around him and slipped a dime into the slot.

Ike looked up at her. She was smiling. Her lips and teeth were blue.

"Go on," she said.

Ike turned the handle. There was a *clink*, and he lifted the silver door.

A yellow gum ball tumbled out.

The bag girl took it from his hand and popped it into her mouth. Her lips and teeth turned green. Then she put another dime in the slot.

"What the heck," she said.

Ike turned the handle again. There was a *clink*. He lifted the door.

"It's a ring!" he said.

"A toad ring," the bag girl said. "I hope that's the one you were trying for."

Ike smiled up at her. "Thanks," he said.

She slapped him on the back. "No sweat, kid," she said.

Ike kept his left hand in his lap during supper. When his mother passed the casserole, he took it with one hand.

"Is something wrong with your hand?" his father asked.

"No," Ike said.

"Then why don't you take the dish with both hands?"

"I don't know," Ike said. "I just feel like holding it one-handed."

After supper Ike and Mem and Debbie

went back out to play. The lightning bugs were floating in the air again, like sparks.

"Come on, Debbie," Mem said. "Let's play in the sandbox. *By ourselves.*"

Ike walked next door to Buzzy's house and knocked on the screen door. Buzzy appeared behind it. He didn't open the door.

"Aren't you coming out?" Ike asked through the screen.

"No," Buzzy said. "I don't want any more of Dave's dumb lightning rings."

"You won't have to take one," Ike said. "I promise."

"Are you going to stand up to him?" Buzzy asked.

"Sort of," Ike said.

Buzzy stepped outside. Ike noticed he had a

bandage on his finger. Buzzy saw Ike looking at it and quickly stuffed his hand into his pocket.

"It's okay," Ike said. He took his hand out of his pocket. "See?"

Buzzy smiled.

"Hey, here he comes," he whispered to Ike. "You do the talking."

Dave walked across the yard and stepped up onto Buzzy's back porch. Hugo was walking at a distance behind him. He stopped behind a tree and peeked around it.

"I can't make lightning rings anymore, guys," Dave said with a sneer. "My big-mouth brother squealed."

Hugo ducked back behind the tree.

Ike looked at Buzzy. Buzzy looked at Ike. They tried not to smile.

"Wait here," Ike said. "I'll be right back."

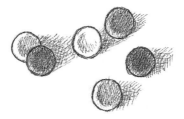

Ike climbed the stairs two at a time. He ran into his room. The lamp beside his bed was on. The six creepy-crawly rings were on the nightstand next to it. Ike scooped them into his pocket, then ran back downstairs.

"Where's the fire?" his father asked as Ike tore through the kitchen.

Ike didn't answer. He ran out the door and back across the yards to Buzzy's porch. He reached into his pocket and pulled out one of the rings.

"Here," he said to Dave, out of breath.

"It's a creepy-crawly lightning ring."

"Whoa!" Dave said. "A glow-in-the-dark spider! *Cool!*" He slid the ring onto his finger.

"I like this kind of lightning ring better than yours," Ike said. He took a step back.

"Me t-too," Buzzy said.

Dave's smile disappeared. He squinted at Ike. He squinted at Buzzy. Then he laughed.

"I like it better too!" he said.

Ike dug back into his pocket and pulled out a ring for Buzzy.

"Thanks," Buzzy said. He tore the bandage off his finger. The yellow-green spot was gone. He slid on the ring. It glowed in the dark. "A snake," he said with a grin.

Ike dug into his pocket again and pulled out another ring.

"Here you go, Hugo," he said. "I have one for you too."

"For me?" Hugo said, peeking around the tree.

"You're giving one to *him*?" Dave asked with a scowl. "Even after he *squealed*?"

"I have enough for everybody," Ike said. "Come get it, Hugo."

Hugo stepped out from behind the tree and ran across the yard to the porch.

"Thanks, Ike," he said. He took the ring and slid it onto his finger. He stuck out his tongue. "Yuck. A slug."

Ike then walked over to the sandbox in his backyard. Mem and Debbie were there, digging a hole.

"Mem," Ike said, "I have something for you."

Mem put her hand to her ear. "Did you

hear something?" she said to Debbie. "I thought I heard a big dummy."

"We're not talking to you," Debbie said to Ike.

Ike dug into his pocket and pulled out two beetle rings.

"Wow!" Debbie said. "Look, Mem! Glow-in-the-dark rings!"

Mem tried not to look, but she peeked anyway. She smiled.

"There's one for each of you," Ike said. "They're creepy-crawly lightning rings."

Debbie took one and slid it onto her finger. "Thanks, Ike!" she said beaming.

Mem took the other one and slid it onto her finger.

"I'm sorry I wore Dave's lightning ring," Ike said. "I shouldn't have."

"Then I guess you're not a big dummy anymore," Mem said.

Ike smiled.

"Look," he said, pointing at Mem's ring. "It's a lightning bug."

Mem looked at it closer.

"It looks like a beetle," she said.

"Lightning bugs *are* beetles," Ike said.

He dug into his pocket and pulled out the last ring. It was the toad ring. He tore off his bandage. The yellow-green spot was gone.

"A toad," Mem said. "Just like Toady!"

Ike slipped the ring onto his finger. Then he dug the gum balls out of his pockets.

"Anybody want a gum ball?" he called out.

Everybody did. They each took a couple and popped them into their mouths. Their cheeks

bulged. Their lips and teeth turned colors. Then they played Living Statues in the grass.

The lightning bugs floated around them while they spun and froze. The bugs didn't float in a circle. They didn't float in a ring. They floated higgledy-piggledy, like sparks.

PATRICK JENNINGS has written several critically acclaimed books for young readers. This is his fourth book about Ike and Mem, following *The Bird Shadow*, *The Tornado Watches*, and *The Weeping Willow*. He lives in Washington State with his family.

ANNA ALTER is a graduate of the Rhode Island School of Design. She illustrated *The Three Little Kittens* and *Estelle and Lucy*, which she also wrote. She lives in Massachusetts.